You're All My Favourites

Sam McBratney

illustrated by Anita Jeram

WALKER BOOKS
AND SUBSIDIARIES
LONDON · BOSTON · SYDNEY · AUCKLAND

Once upon a time

there was a mother bear,

a father bear

and three baby bears.

A first baby bear.   A second baby bear.

And a third baby bear.

Whoever tucked them in at night

always said the same thing to them:

"You are the most wonderful baby bears

in the whole wide world!"

One night, after their Mummy Bear

had tucked them in, and after she had said

"You are the most wonderful baby bears

in the whole wide world",

the baby bears began to wonder.

"But how do you know?" they asked

their Mummy Bear. "How do you know

we are the most wonderful baby bears

in the whole wide world?"

"Because your daddy told me,"

said their Mummy Bear.

"When your daddy saw you on the night

that you were born, he said —

and I remember it very well — he said,

'Those are the nicest baby bears

I have ever seen.

They are the nicest baby bears

anyone has ever seen!'"

That was a good answer.
The three baby bears snuggled
down as content as could be.

But one day, the first baby bear

began to think. He wondered if the

other two bears were better than he was.

They had patches, after all,

and he did not. Maybe his mummy

really really liked patches.

And the second baby bear began to wonder.

Maybe daddy loves the other two

more than me, she thought.

They were boy bears, after all,

and she was not.

And the third baby bear

began to worry.

I'm only the littlest, he thought.

Everybody's bigger than me!

So that night the three baby bears asked their Daddy Bear,

"But which one of us do you like most?

Who is your favourite?

We can't all be the best."

"Yes you can," said their Daddy Bear. "I know you can

because I heard your mummy say so. When she saw you"

— and Daddy Bear picked up the first baby bear

to give him a cuddle — "she said,

'That is the most perfect first little

bear that anyone has ever seen.'"

"Even with no patches?"

"Patches don't matter at all,"

replied his daddy,

as he tucked him in.

"And when your mummy saw you" – Daddy Bear picked up the second baby bear – "she said, 'That is the most perfect second little bear that anyone has ever seen.'"

"Even if I'm not a boy?"

"Girl or boy, it makes no difference," said her daddy, and he hugged her tight.

"And when your mummy saw you" – Daddy Bear

lifted the last baby bear into his arms –

"she said, 'That is the most perfect third

little bear that anyone has ever seen.'"

"Even if I'm the littlest?"

"Biggly or littley,

we love you just the same.

So there. Three favourites.

You're all my favourites!"

And the best baby bears in the whole wide world

went to sleep as happily as could be, because

that was a good answer too.

For all *my* favourites:
Sam and Daniel and Jack
and Adam and Ella   ~ S. M^{c}B.

For Joe, Danny and Kitty   ~ A. J.

First published 2004 by Walker Books Ltd
87 Vauxhall Walk, London SE11 5HJ

This edition published 2007

2 4 6 8 10 9 7 5 3

Text © 2004 Sam McBratney
Illustrations © 2004 Anita Jeram

The right of Sam McBratney and Anita Jeram to be identified
as author and illustrator respectively of this work has been asserted by them
in accordance with the Copyright, Designs and Patents Act 1988.

This book has been typeset in Mrs Eaves

Printed in China

British Library Cataloguing in Publication Data:
a catalogue record for this book is available from the British Library.

ISBN 978-1-84428-515-0

www.walker.co.uk